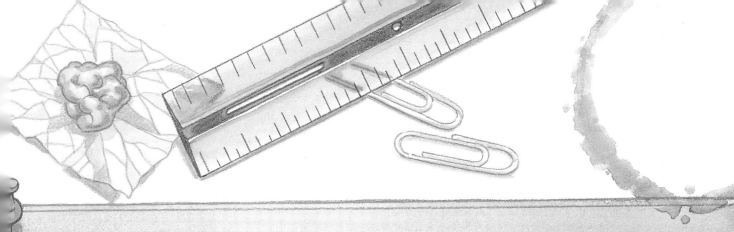

THE GOOCH MACHINE
Poems for Children to Perform

PROJECT:	PLAN A:	SIZE	AUTHORIZED BY:	DESIGNER:	LAYOUT:
Gooch Machine	PRODUCTION	8.5 x 11	B. Bagert & B.M.P	T. Ellis	T. Gilbe

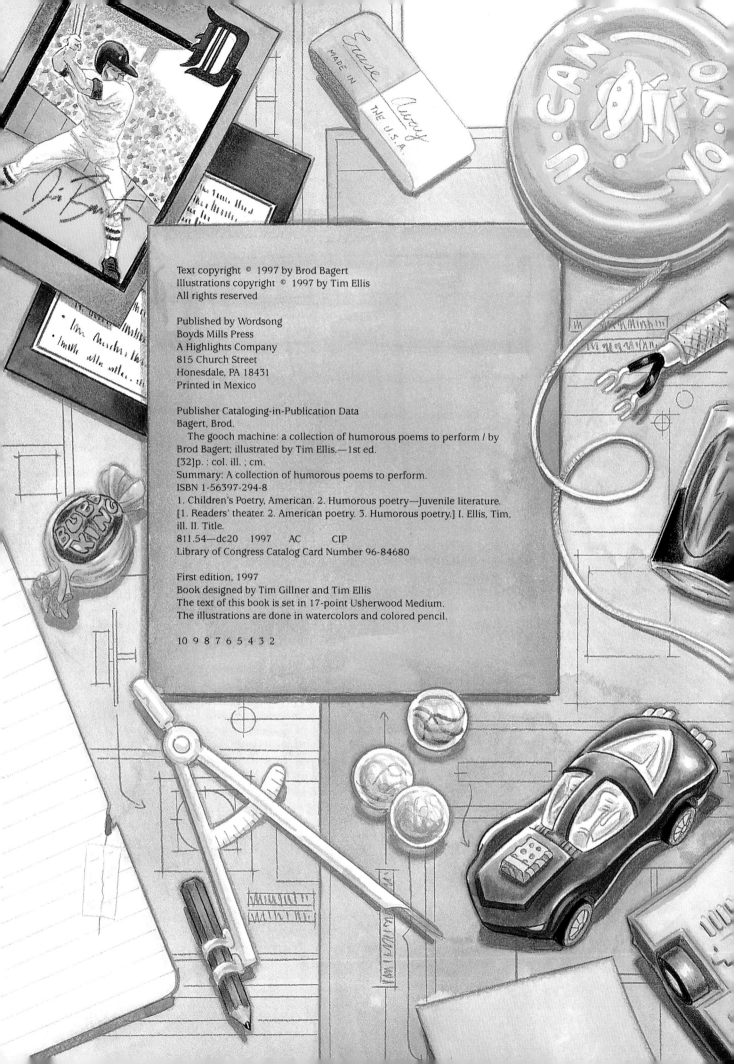

Published by Wordsong
Boyds Mills Press
A Highlights Company
815 Church Street
Honesdale, PA 18431
Printed in Mexico

Publisher Cataloging-in-Publication Data
Bagert, Brod.
    The gooch machine: a collection of humorous poems to perform / by
Brod Bagert; illustrated by Tim Ellis.—1st ed.
[32]p. : col. ill. ; cm.
Summary: A collection of humorous poems to perform.
ISBN 1-56397-294-8
1. Children's Poetry, American. 2. Humorous poetry—Juvenile literature.
[1. Readers' theater. 2. American poetry. 3. Humorous poetry.] I. Ellis, Tim,
ill. II. Title.
811.54—dc20   1997   AC   CIP
Library of Congress Catalog Card Number 96-84680

First edition, 1997
Book designed by Tim Gillner and Tim Ellis
The text of this book is set in 17-point Usherwood Medium.
The illustrations are done in watercolors and colored pencil.

10 9 8 7 6 5 4 3 2

THE GOOCH MACHINE
Poems for Children to Perform

by Brod Bagert
Illustrated by Tim Ellis

Wordsong
Boyds Mills Press

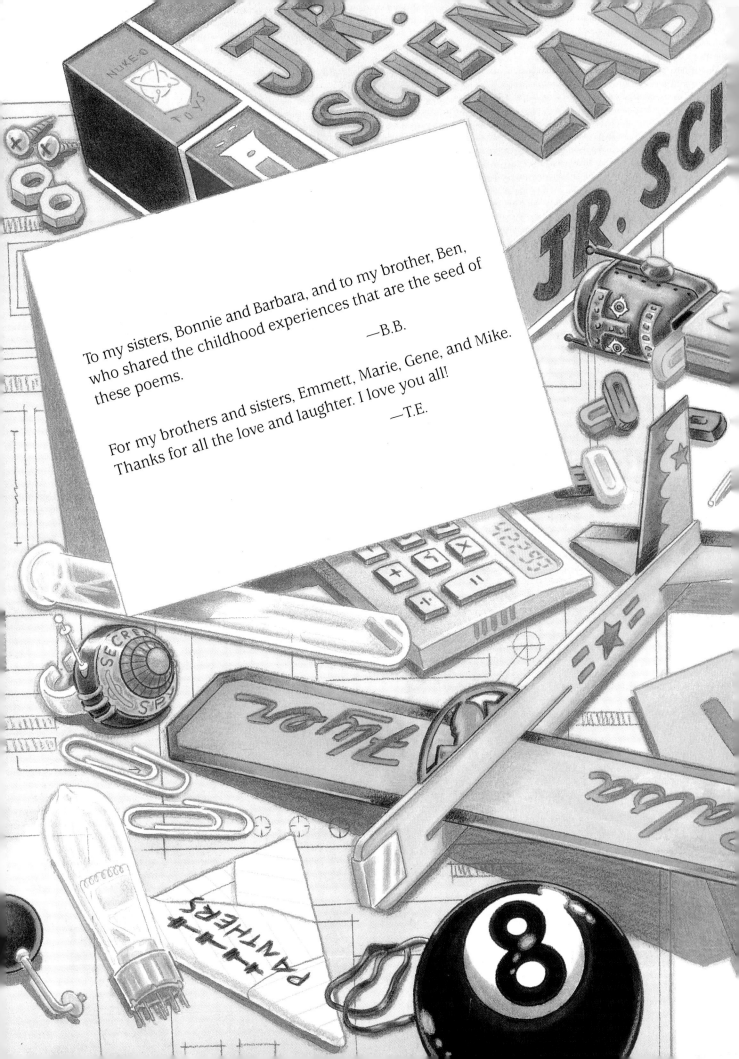

To my sisters, Bonnie and Barbara, and to my brother, Ben, who shared the childhood experiences that are the seed of these poems.

—B.B.

For my brothers and sisters, Emmett, Marie, Gene, and Mike. Thanks for all the love and laughter. I love you all!

—T.E.

TABLE OF CONTENTS

To My Young Reader

When I wrote these poems, I imagined your voice saying the words out loud with lots of expression. So please, don't just read these poems. Perform them like an actor on the stage. That way you'll hear the poems the way I hear them.

Here's a hint about reading with expression: If you want expression in the sound of your voice, all you have to do is put expression on your face. To make your voice sound happy, smile as you say the words. To sound sad, make a sad face. Give it a try. You are going to be a terrific performer.

Author's Note To Parents and Teachers

Those of us who love poetry have felt its power to enrich. Sadly, we are few. I yearn for a world in which we are many. The thrust of this collection is to help broaden the number of children who experience poetry in their lives.

Because children like to laugh, most of these poems tend to be funny. Children also enjoy quiet moments, so there are quiet poems here, too. Whatever the tone, be it silly or somber, these poems are about what children feel, and I believe the emotions of child-hood are a serious matter.

I also believe that poems are best experienced when read aloud, so I try to write poems that encourage children to perform. Each poem occurs in an implied dramatic setting and speaks in a child's voice. As children perform such poems and act out their own feelings, they begin to understand those feelings more deeply, they learn to laugh at themselves, and they grow. It's a simple recipe—a dash of drama, a pinch of emotion, a sprinkle of good humor.

I have a favorite passage from this book. It occurs on page thirty-two at the end of the last poem: *Or do they live forever,/ With green grass and blue skies,/ Like the flame of poet-fire/ When it burns in children's eyes.* These words contain the passion of my life, for I believe the fire of poetry, ignited in the child, will burn in the adult and pass from generation to generation. I hope these poems help you light that fire.

Perfect Children

We children are sweet.
We children are nice.
We always say "please"
At least once, maybe twice.

Our voices are gentle,
Like a beautiful song . . .
If you think this is true
You are totally wrong!

Countdown Jitters

Ten . . . Nine . . . Eight . . .
Wait!

Seven . . . Six . . .
Five . . . Four . . .
You count real well
But don't count more.

Three . . . Two . . .
What can I do?

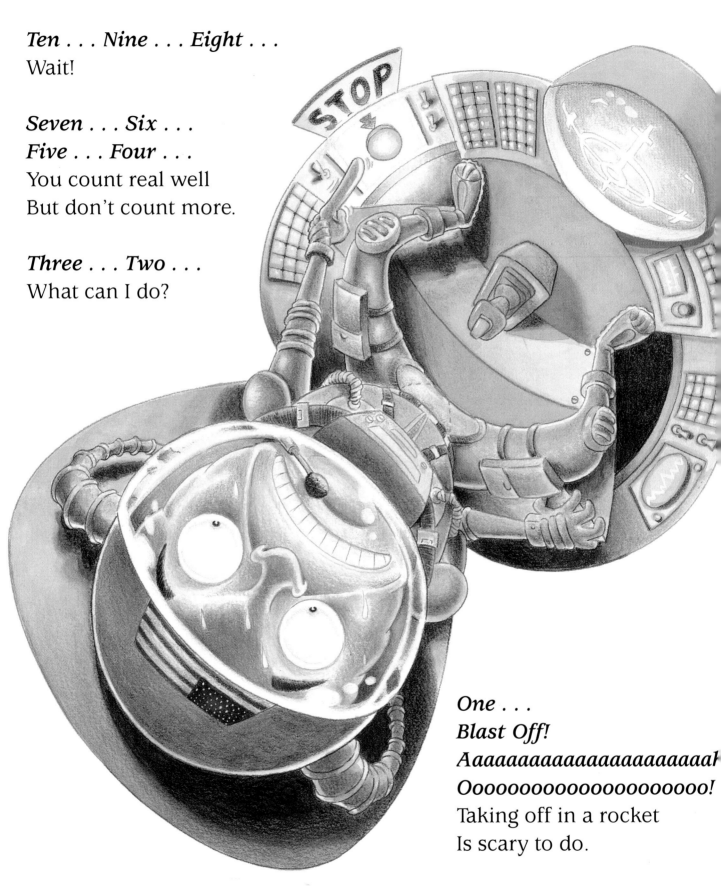

One . . .
Blast Off!
Aaaaaaaaaaaaaaaaaaaaaaaaaaah
Oooooooooooooooooooooo!
Taking off in a rocket
Is scary to do.

Alien Eyes?

Our galaxy is a billion stars
Afloat in an endless sea,
Like a tiny drop of cream
In a giant cup of tea.
So many stars in that ocean,
Oh surely there must be
Some other eyes
That search night skies
And wonder about me.

Donut-Fingers

She said, "Do not lick your fingers!"
And I know I never should,
But the sugar on these donuts
Makes my fingers taste so good.

I see drippy jelly filling
Mixed with crispy donut-crumbs,
And I'm licking on my fingers,
And I'm sucking on my thumbs.

How can a kid resist?
Sticky fingers taste so sweet.
So for now I'll just be glad
I don't eat donuts with my feet.

Sisters

This is not my shoe,
And this shirt is much too big.
It's not my mess! It's her mess!
My sister is the pig!

I straightened up my room,
I neatly made my bed,
I organized my closet,
I work hard to stay ahead.

But to you it doesn't matter.
Why is it you can't see?
My sister is the messy one.
Why do you pick on me?

She's the one who's noisy!
She's the one who's wild!
Remember me? Your favorite?
Your "Perfect Angel" child.

Lost and Found

There he is!
He looked this way!
He's smiling and he sees me!
Oh boy, I'm found
Swept off the ground
Please, Dad, don't ever leave me.

Sometimes I argue with my dad,
He always wants his way,
But snuggled here in Daddy's arms
Is where I want to stay.

Dad's Greatest Fear

Sometimes my dad gets worried,
His face looks sad and grim,
I guess he's scared that someday
I'll grow up just like him.

The Homework Guarantee

I would have done it yesterday
If it weren't for the rain,
All that lightning and thunder
Are so tricky on my brain.

And I'd like to work real hard tonight
To raise my grades right out of sight,
But my finger has a splinter,
And it hurts me when I write.

Now tomorrow is another day
So we'll have to wait and see,
I intend to do my homework
But there's still no guarantee.

I know I've got to do it
If I want to grow up smart,
But something always happens
Every time I try to start.

2 + 2

I know that two plus two is four,
But so is one plus three.
Now someone please explain to me
How such a thing can be?

And then there's four plus zero,
And the answer's four again.
Why not some other number
Like seven, eight, or ten?

I'm going to learn to add
But it's such a crazy task.
How can the answer be the same
When a different question's asked?

Sound Advice

I asked the jazzman if he could say
What instrument I should learn to play.
The trombone, the saxophone,
The lead guitar, the base?
But the jazzman only shook his head.
Then he made a funny face and said,
    "Listen close and open your eyes.
    You young cats got to realize
    That everything is synthesized
    Now that the sound is digitized.
    If you want to get a gig
    That ain't gonna go away,
    Multimedia computer
    Is the instrument to play."

Wolfgang Rock

If Mozart were alive
He'd be playing lead guitar,
Dancing in the spotlight
And prancing like a star.
His hair would be dyed purple
And his music would be bold.
If Mozart were alive
He'd be playing rock-'n'-roll.

The Food Cheer

Carnivores! Carnivores!
We eat meat!

Herbivores! Herbivores!
Plants taste sweet!

Omnivores! Omnivores!
Hear us sing—
We eat almost everything!

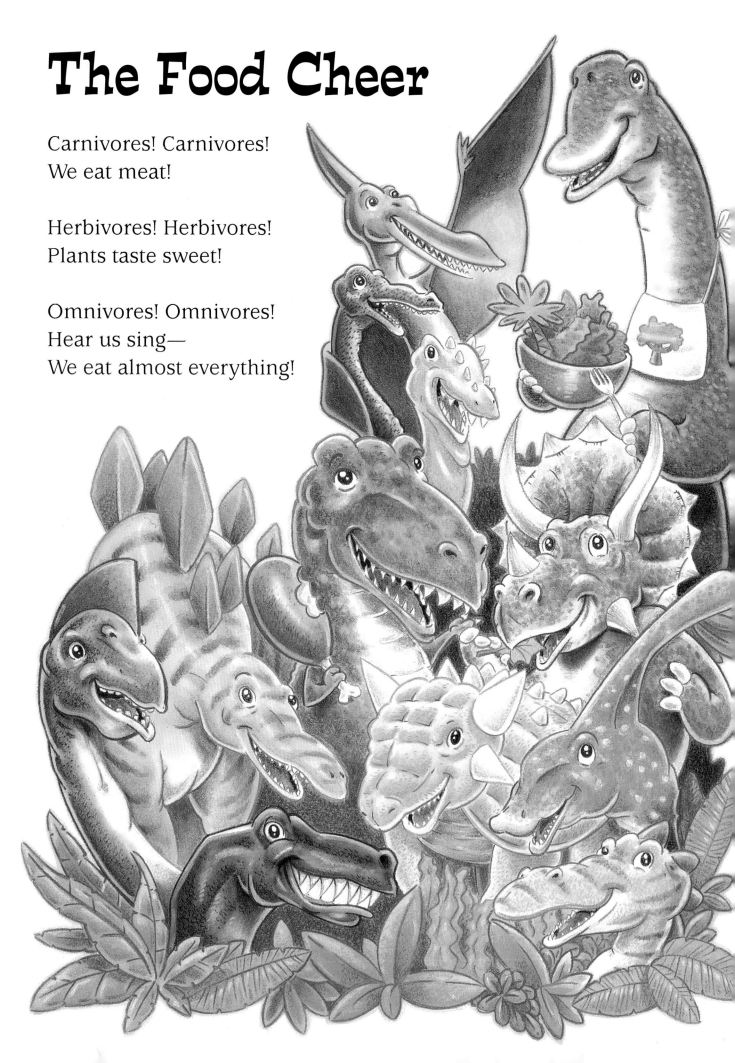

Buzzard-Truth

If a buzzard in the desert
Stops to ask you how you feel,
Tell him, "Fine! I feel fine!"
Or you might be his next meal.

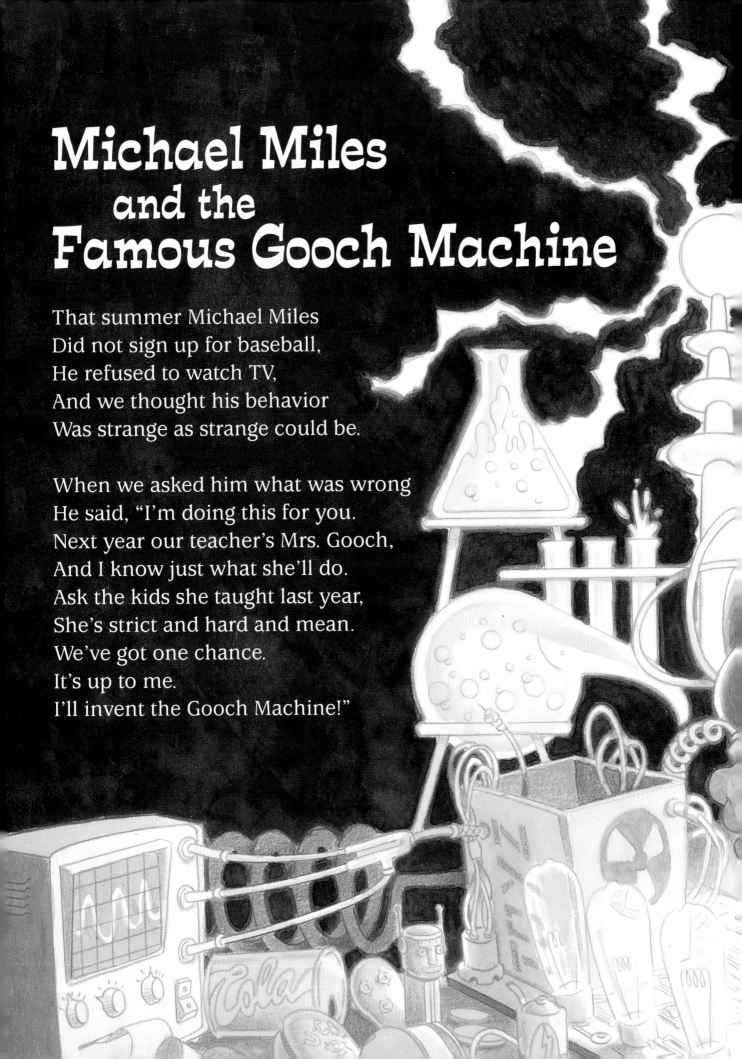

Michael Miles
and the
Famous Gooch Machine

That summer Michael Miles
Did not sign up for baseball,
He refused to watch TV,
And we thought his behavior
Was strange as strange could be.

When we asked him what was wrong
He said, "I'm doing this for you.
Next year our teacher's Mrs. Gooch,
And I know just what she'll do.
Ask the kids she taught last year,
She's strict and hard and mean.
We've got one chance.
It's up to me.
I'll invent the Gooch Machine!"

He hung a sign on his bedroom door:
Danger! Stay Away!
Gooch Machine Experiments
Are Going on Today!
He stayed locked up for hours.
He worked real late at night.
His skin grew pale,
His nails grew long,
His hair a frazzled sight.
He groaned and moaned and grumbled
And threw pencils on the floor.
Lightning flashed . . .
Test tubes bubbled . . .
And smoke poured out the door.

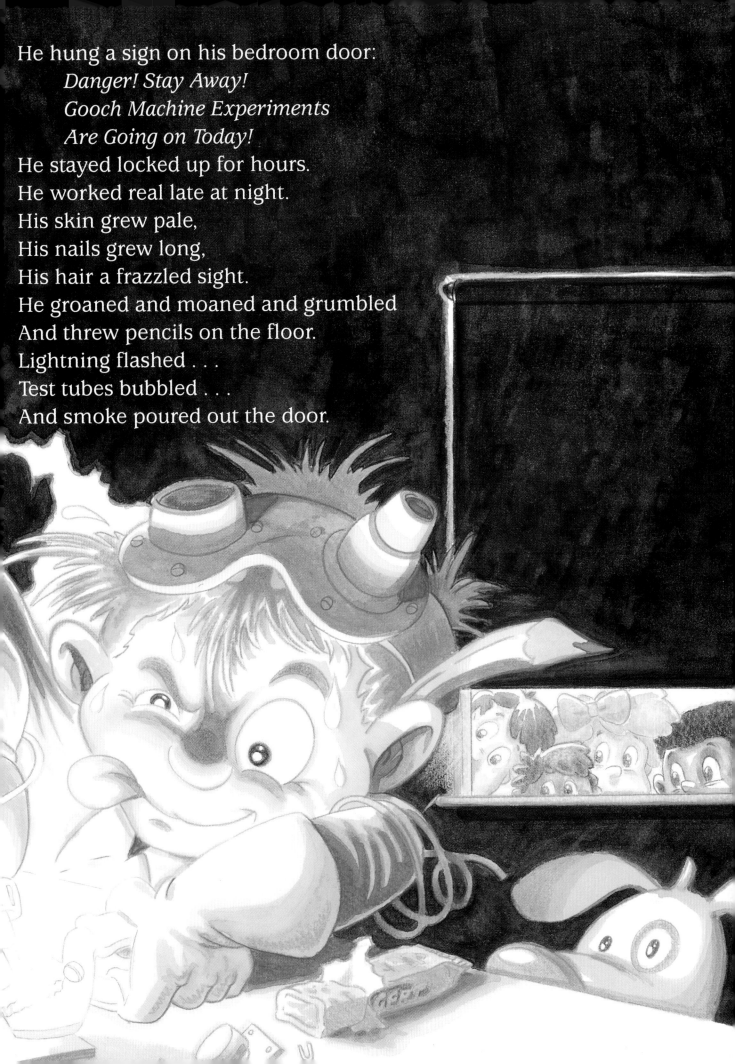

It lasted all that summer
But when September finally came,
Michael Miles said, "Present!"
When the teacher called his name.

And there she was, Mrs. Gooch,
Looking big and mean,
But somehow that year, Mrs. Gooch
Was never what she seemed.

Whenever she got angry
And was about to scream,
She would sigh instead and tilt her head
As if walking in a dream.

Then she'd smile at us so gently
And talk lovingly and slow,
And no one noticed Michael
Pushing buttons with his toe.

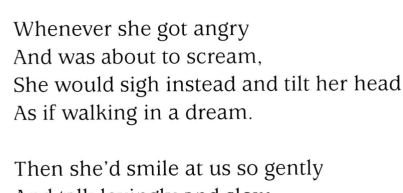

It was a small black box with two red buttons
As simple as could be,
But it could change a teacher's mood
As quick as one-two-three.

That Gooch Machine was so much fun
We knew we had to share,
So we made a thousand more,
And we sent them everywhere!

So if some day your teacher smiles
And begins to hug her book,
You're sure to find a Gooch Machine
If you stop and take a look.

Hh Ii Jj Kk Ll Mm Nn Oo

Ms. Bronson's Class

Hidden somewhere in your classroom,
Very close to someone's feet,
A Gooch Machine is working hard
To keep your teacher sweet.

Our Country's Quilt

We had very little to keep us warm
Against the coming winter storm,
Just a pile of worn-out rags
Tattered, torn and stuffed in bags.
   A blue silk shirt,
   A gabardine coat,
   Beaded buckskin and a cotton shawl,
   A calico dress, some old wool pants,
   And a lace mantilla from a costume ball.
There was lots more cloth from which to choose
But each piece was too small to use.

So we gathered what we had,
While remaining very calm,
And we cut each patch in a special shape
To reveal its special charm,
Then we snipped and sewed and stitched,
And we all danced arm in arm,
To celebrate this country quilt
We made to keep us warm.

The Poem on My Pillow

The house was dark,
And I felt a little scared,
But those cookies kept calling from the kitchen,
So I tiptoed down the stairs
And peeked around the corner
To make sure there were no monsters.

Then I saw my dad,
Alone at the kitchen table
With an open book
And a pencil and paper.
He wrote very carefully.
Then he stopped . . .
And he listened . . .
And he smiled.
This morning
I found this poem on my pillow.

To the Little Boy Who Hides

I listen for your breath while you sleep,
I follow your footsteps across the floor above me,
I hear the creak of wooden steps as you tiptoe down,
And I feel your fear of the dark.
Oh, little son,
When you tremble in the night,
Listen for the beat of your heart . . .
It pounds with the courage of the ages,
And that courage will make its own light.

When I read the poem I thought,
He heard me!
Was he angry?
Did he think I had been bad?
Then I noticed how he signed the poem . . .

To my son . . .
With love . . .
From Dad

Good Models

E. Dickinson

W. Whitman

E. Browning

I read my first poem
And I felt like frowning,
It sounded too much
Like Elizabeth Browning.

Then in my next poem
I felt myself change,
Into Emily Dickinson—
Quiet and strange.

Now it happened again,
Please don't think I'm weird,
But today I'm Walt Whitman,
Without the long beard.

As I read all my poems
I discover a rule,
I write like the poets
We're reading at school.

The Poet-Tree

One day I saw a cypress tree
With knees just like the knees on me.
I saw a pine tree tall and green
That made the air feel fresh and clean.
I saw a giant oak,
And a quiet, stately palm,
With leaves like fans to cool the sky
In places where it's warm.
But in all the world, from pole to pole,
My eyes may never see
Branches with leaves that sing to me
Like my lovely poet-tree.

Butterfly Fire

How long do butterflies live?
Two days?
Two weeks?
Two years?
Do they have quiet butterfly funerals,
And cry tiny butterfly tears?
Or do they live forever,
With green grass and blue skies,
Like the flame of poet-fire
When it burns in children's eyes.